Stevie Tenderheart©

My Favorite Place to be...

(A Coloring Book)

Vera
It's okay to
color OUTSIDE
The LINES of
Life!

Love

Written
by
Steve Laible

Colored
by
The Incredible

____

Stevie Tenderheart©
My Favorite Place to be...
(A Coloring Book)

Written
by
Steve Laible

©

Copyright 2010
Worldwide Rights Reserved

New York	New Zealand	Hong Kong	Mexico City	Johannesburg	Tokyo
Ashland	Pismo Beach	Coos Bay	Grants Pass	Empire	Dublin
Paris	Copenhagen	London	Sydney	New Delhi	Toronto

FIRST EDITION

Stevie Likeness Designed by Chase Howard Laible
Formatted for Publication by Tom Piper
Drawings by Nancy Watson

Published by
The Kodel Group

Empire Holdings - Literary Division for Young Readers
P.O. Box 38, Grants Pass, Oregon, USA 97528

Summary: A little boy who simply loves his bed and wishes he could take it everywhere he goes.

ISBN: 978-0-9844784-1-5

Printed in the United States of America.

PREFACE

It is with sad regret that children do not remain "children" for longer than they do. So it is our job, as parents, to buy them another year or two. It is my belief that children should remain children for as long as possible. Through my stories, I hope to nurture their imaginations for as long as possible. And a note to you moms: I know you like to color too, but remember to "share" your Stevie Tenderheart Coloring Book. (BIG SMILE)

DEDICATIONS

I dedicate this coloring book to all of you aspiring artists and authors and dreamers who are only about five or six. Let nothing distract you from happiness and always believe in yourselves. You make this world a better place. Follow your heart and follow your dreams. Choose integrity as your true north and you will never get lost. And remember this most, A Change of Heart Changes Everything.

Captain Tenderheart

ACKNOWLEDGEMENTS

To the incredible Nancy Watson, thank you for working so hard to produce such wonderful, expressive illustrations; and for helping me tell my story about a little boy who simply loves his bed and wishes he could take it everywhere he goes. Nancy, we've created art that is beautiful and fun. Now let's sit back and watch the children grin as they help their mommies color this wonderful book in.

FOREWORD

I was only about five or six when my parents brightened the night. Just before bed on a Sunday night; just after my bath and before my favorite show—they sat me down and said, "Disneyland", and that's all that I know.

Whatever else followed after that opening statement was lost. My brain was advancing much faster than I...was I really going to Disneyland? Was it a dream come true? Sometimes when things get this good, it doesn't seem real; not meant for kids like me but for kids like you.

I was beyond excitement and I could not sleep. Not for days and not for weeks. But eventually I was there. I was in the Magic Kingdom.

While tired from the three-day ride in the back of the family car, I have but a blurry recollection of a few nights in wayside motels. But before I knew it, the moment was finally here. I was standing inside the hallowed gates of Disneyland watching a parade pass by. I was not aware this was a make-believe town; it looked pretty real to me.

It was very clean and everything was painted so nice. I do remember that. The sights and sounds and sweet smells; the people crowded in together on every inch of ground. I was so excited and quite spellbound. There was so much to take in. I was in fairytale land and I didn't even know what that meant. All that I saw, I believed as real, and that's really the premise of this story of innocence.

Being on the streets of Disneyland was like being at a big block party. I remember lots of noises and horns and happy yells. So many costumes; everyone in the parade looked great. There was dancing in the streets and everyone was happy and smiling.

There were so many children on the shoulders of their fathers. Perched so tall to help them see it all. I'd never seen that before. I had never once been on my father's shoulders. But then again, why would I? There was not much I could not see for myself back at home. I had wondered though, why hadn't my mommy tugged on my daddy's arm and asked him to lift me up. All I could see were pockets and belts. Lots and lots of pockets and belts!

Maybe my parents knew something I didn't. (Imagine that.) Maybe I was left standing on the ground for a very good reason. Maybe it was fate. And then sure enough, that's when something happened that was great—once in a lifetime great! It was so real it felt unreal. Does that make any sense? At the age of only five or six, you really can't explain why your head gets dizzy or feels like a dream when you see something you can't explain.

This very neat, old-fashioned convertible car, with spoke wheels, stopped right in front of me. A man in a tan suit stepped down and out of the car and came right over to me. The hand-waving and brightly lit smiles and noise grew much louder now. There was more excitement in the air now than ever.

This man stopped and looked me square in the eyes. The crowd grew quiet. Everyone's eyes were now trained on this man standing straight in front of me. His face was very familiar looking. (Like maybe a friend or an uncle, at one of my mother's family or high school class reunions or something. She used to always drag me along and show me off.) But his grandfatherly smile was more familiar than that. He came right up to me and spoke and patted my head but I do not remember what he said.

And then it dawned on me, who this man was. His thin mustache curved up and his smile gave it away. I had seen this man before. But not so close up or in person before. As the crowd closed in around us, I got to see more.

He kneeled down and shook my tiny little hand and then said something more. (And for the life of me, I really do need to start listening more.) He again patted my head, then stood up and walked away. As he disappeared into the crowd, everyone could see the huge commotion. All I could see were the backsides of people again. But for that one moment in time, I was standing right there, toe-to-toe, with the real Walt Disney. He had touched my head and knighted me that day.

This is the man I watched on television every Sunday night, in my pajamas, after my bath. He was the one who knew everyone. He was speaking to me that day, just as he does when he introduces the Wonderful World of Disney on our family's black and white tv.

I had never seen anyone from television in person before. But then why would I? Television was only invented a few years before. But hearing his soft-spoken, gentle laugh that day, even I could tell I was near greatness. I was so excited and beyond belief. Surely this is how Donald and Mickey and Goofy must have felt, the first time they met him too.

But here's the most important part of my little story. Standing right next to Mr. Disney, but just a few steps to the side, was this beautiful fairytale creature that had come alive. She is still imprinted in my mind. Wearing a pretty blue and white dress, I remember every detail from her puffy shoulders to her long white stockings. I even remember her shiny, buckled black shoes and boy did she smell swell. She had the most beautiful long blonde hair that I had ever seen; the rosiest cheeks and the prettiest smile there had ever been. And she was smiling right at me.

To this day, I cannot remember what she said either, but it was probably something about me being a most darling and handsome young lad. This truly was the most beautiful girl in the whole wide-world and she was standing right there, in front of me. And when she spoke to me in her beautiful voice, I more than melted. There were like bluebirds in my heart, singing and stuff. I was standing toe-to-toe with Alice in Wonderland—the "real" one!

(Lest you forget, I was a very young lad of only five or six. I still believed in cowboys and horsey sticks.) All that I saw was real. Such was the innocence of a youth not yet spilled.

Then to my surprise and sheer delight, Alice in Wonderland leaned in and kissed me good-night. She kissed me! Right there on my face; on my left cheek to be exact. Her lips cast a spell as the crowd began to swell. As mothers and others awed and sighed, my Nana stepped up and snapped a picture before I cried. A photo I still have with me today. I was embarrassed and in love at the same time. It was a great feeling—one that I never forgot.

I can tell you this, and I know this for a fact, this was the precise moment in time, of my young life, where I can share with you the meaning of life. For this is when I learned the beauty of love at-first-sight; just as my parents had, five or six years before this magical night.

I was imprinted for life with my fascination for blondes — Teri Hatcher and Diane Lane—notwithstanding. I am also in love with these beautiful women too, but I am no longer five or six (more like 56) and I think there are laws against this. (BIG WINK) But when you are only five or six, you believe in everything until otherwise informed! This is part of the charm.

In my case, I really had met Walt Disney and Alice in Wonderland really did kiss me...

Stevie Tenderheart ©

Stevie Fan Club

(Online Store)

Free Shipping

www.stevietenderheart.com

Stevie Dolls, "Change of Heart" & "Stevie" Bracelets
T-Shirts, Hats, Kites, Stickers, Patches

Stevie Tenderheart Collection Series
Next in the Series
Wait a Minute!

A Change of _____ _____ Changes Everything ©

Made in the USA
Columbia, SC
03 March 2019